IF YOU LIVED HERE YOU'D BE HOME BY NOW

ED BRIANT

A NEAL PORTER BOOK ROARING BROOK PRESS NEW YORK

DOOF

CRASH

THUD.

CLANG!

BUY
FIT-RITE
SALE
SHOP'N'DROP
BARGAIN
SALE
SALE
SALE

SALE

FIT-RITE
FIT-RITE
BUY
SALE
SHOPNDROP
BARGAIN
SHOPPER
SALE
SALE
SALE

SNAP